Cuddle Bear's BOOK OF Hugs

Claire Freedman   Gavin Scott

LITTLE TIGER
LONDON

Cuddle Bear LOVES giving hugs,
And bringing cuddly cheer.
But one bear can't hug everyone,
So here's his **great idea**...

HUG ACADEMY

"A school for little bears!" he cheers.
"My **Hug Academy!**
I teach them all my cuddling skills.
Come, peep inside and see!"

"In Cuddle Class," says Cuddle Bear,
"We learn what **hugs** can do.
They **cheer** you up! They make you **smile**,
When you've been feeling **blue!**"

Then Cuddle Bear calls,
"Practice time!

Now, find a
partner, please!

Let's keep it light,
don't hold too **tight**-

A **cuddle**,
not a **squeeze!**"

The bears must all keep **fit** and **strong**,

They work out in the **gym**,

And even **whales** might need a **hug**,

So each bear learns to **swim**.

They practise on an **octopus**,
To get used to the **tickles**.

And **porcupines** need special care,

Because of all their prickles!

Giraffes are **very** hard to reach,
But they **still** need a cuddle.
Frogs are small and **slippery** -
Bears could get in a **muddle**!

Whatever **size**, whatever shape,
From teeny up to **tall**,
Or growly, fluffy, bouncy, shy –
There is a hug for all.

Today at last, it's hug **exams**!
The eager bears make sure
They show off all their cuddling skills
To get a **super** score!

Ready, teddy, cuddle!

"**Well done!**" says Cuddle Bear with pride,
"You **ALL** have passed the test.
    You've earned a yellow heart that proves
    Your cuddles are the **BEST!**"

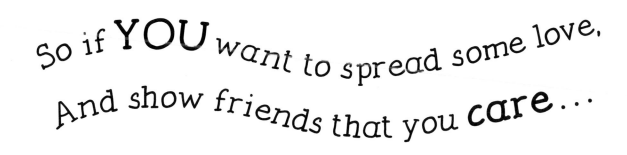

So if **YOU** want to spread some love,
And show friends that you **care**...

...Give someone close a cuddle now,

As hugs are made to SHARE!

To Mark and Ruth with lots of love
~ C F

For Vics, Laurie and Frida
~ G S ·

LITTLE TIGER PRESS LTD
an imprint of the Little Tiger Group,
1 Coda Studios, 189 Munster Road, London SW6 6AW
www.littletiger.co.uk
First published in Great Britain 2018

Text copyright © Claire Freedman 2018
Illustrations copyright © Gavin Scott 2018